BIG HERO 6

TEAM-UP!

By Laura Hitchcock
Illustrated by the Disney Storybook Art Team

A Random House PICTUREBACK® Book

Random House 🏠 New York

Copyright © 2014 Disney Enterprises, Inc. All rights reserved. Published in the United States by Random House Children's Books,
a division of Random House LLC, 1745 Broadway, New York, NY 10019, and in Canada by Random House of Canada Limited,
Toronto, Penguin Random House Companies, in conjunction with Disney Enterprises, Inc. Pictureback, Random House,
and the Random House colophon are registered trademarks of Random House LLC.
randomhousekids.com
ISBN 978-0-7364-3244-3
Printed in the United States of America
10 9 8 7 6 5 4 3 2 1

. . . Hiro. Hard to tell from looking at him, but this kid is a **ROBOTICS GENIUS**. One day, his inventions will change the world!

Hiro has a nurse-bot named Baymax. He takes care of us and is super helpful. But I was the one who suggested we should all team up!

OuR team could benefit fRom some upGRades.

Hiro wasted no time. He created all kinds of tech stuff for each of us, based on our unique **strengths** and **talents**.

Honey Lemon is a master of chemistry.
Her purse is packed with chemicals that can be combined
to create all sorts of wacky weapons, like this super-sticky
foam that stops villains in their tracks!

Go Go Tomago's super suit has cool discs she can race on—after she practices a bit more! The discs can also be used as weapons—**they're razor-sharp**.

Baymax has **thrusters** and **wings** so he can fly.

I fail to see how flying helps my patients.

His takeoff was a little shaky, but then ... he really took off!

My hand is gone.

Baymax also has a powerful **rocket fist**!

Hiro saved the best for last.
He gave me this amazing suit!

Villains, beware! Evil doesn't stand a chance against us. **We are Big Hero 6!**